4

6

12

14

I didn't know Tansy had a boyfriend.

Yeah! He goes to school at the Crypazalo... Crypsa Zooey Lalis... Cryptee...

The Crypto-Zoological Institute of Atlantis.

Krip-toe-zew-uh-loj-i-kul.

They are one of the sponsors of the circus. They **study and preserve** mythological and magical creatures.

AND RIDE DRAGONS!

Ha! There you go, Sweetums. Maybe **HE** can get you a dragon!

18

Well, one of these days I'll take you with me when I visit Wyatt at the CIA.

Maybe you'll get a chance to see the dragons being fed or something!

That is going to be the best! I can't wait! Maybe I can play with a baby dragon!

23

Magic Trixie, focus on the task! To transmogrify with a wandering mind can have disastrous results.

A week later...

THE GREAT
TREE

MONSTER SOKKI
SCHOOL

LOCH LAKE
LAGOON

MON
SC

Sticky shoe
tape, please, Mr.
Mc Gumm!

Ahem!

Check *this* out!

You *can't fool us!* Your mimi probably **bought** you that at the **circus**, duh. You can get those glittery things anywhere they sell *cheap dragon junk!* I betcha **McGumm** has them in **this** wagon right *now!*

...Tansy's boyfriend works with dragons and when I visited I got this scale...

And before you ask, the answer is no. I have lots of crazy stuff for sale in this wagon, but, kid, a dragon ain't one of them!

I knew you were going to say that.

35

So, I saw the **DRAA-gons** at the circus when I went with Mimi...

Mmmm-hmmm.

That must have been exciting. Dragons are rare and wild creatures.

Besides, you already have a pet.

But a dragon is THE **BESTEST PET** OF ALL!

But...

The next morning...

Do you like them? You LOOK SO cute!!

When you are finished here, sweetie, please transmogrify Abby's diaper and tuck her in for her nap.

Thank you!

Yeesh, he sure knows how to take all the fun out of transmogrification.

So...

...as I was saying...

41

What?
Wait, *no!*
I wasn't
ready...

? Abby? Is that you?

Holy flyin' monkeys! I didn't make a new dragon, I just transmogrified you into one!

MAGIC TRIXIE! WHAT was that noise?

um! UM! I am just... *burping the baby!*

Yeah! Boy, Abby Cadabra, you should not drink your brew so fast, you are making **rude** noises!

...

Awesome!

I've got a dragon, which I wanted real bad. She didn't cost a lot of money, she fits in the house and even has her own room! She will be a cinch to take care of...

CRASH

Whoa, Abby! You got a tail! Careful, okay?

Here!

Dragons have wings, silly, remember?

What are we gonna do, Scratches?

...?

Scratches? C'mon out, buddy!

We gotta find that dragon!

Hmmm. Where'd that guy get to?

C'mon, you guys!

!

The onliest way you are gonna see a dragon is at this circus.

70

Oh...you are in *BIG* trouble.

No duh! Got any suggestions?

Change her back?

And make her tigerburgers?

Plus I need to concentrate with no distractions and it's really distracty around here!

And we can't just open the cage and let her go because she is still a dragon and will fly away...

Or maybe we can... *C'mon!* I just had a great idea!

Ready?

I hope this works...

AND STAY OUT!

It's Magic Trixie!

Magic Trixie is a dragonrider!

later...

Night, honey, see you in the mornin'.

NOW for your bath, Abby, you are unusually dirty today...

Well, everything worked out fine in the end, pal.

I learned my lesson, Abby's Abby again, you're still my bestest bud, a dragon is a drag, and best of all---no one is the wiser...

RING RING

The End

Don't miss the other Magic Trixie books!

Harper Trophy® is a registered trademark of HarperCollins Publishers.

Magic Trixie and the Dragon • Copyright © 2009 by Jill Thompson

All rights reserved. Manufactured in China. No part of this book may be used or reproduced in any manner whatsoever without written permission except in the case of brief quotations embodied in critical articles and reviews. For information address HarperCollins Children's Books, a division of HarperCollins Publishers, 10 East 53rd Street, New York, NY 10022.

www.harpercollinschildrens.com

Library of Congress Cataloging-in-Publication Data • Thompson, Jill, 1966–

Magic Trixie and the dragon / Jill Thompson. -- 1st Harper Trophy ed. • p. cm.

Summary: Magic Trixie, a young witch, wants a real dragon for a pet, but finds that getting one is not as easy as she thought.

ISBN 978-0-06-117050-8 (pbk. bdg.)

1. Graphic novels. [1. Graphic novels. 2. Magic--fiction. 3. Witches--fiction. 4. Dragons--fiction.] I. Title.

PZ7.7.T52Mag 2009 741.5'973--dc22 2008027473

Lettering font created by Jason Arthur from hand lettering by Jill Thompson • ❖ • First Edition

14 15 16 SCP 10 9 8 7 6 5 4